LEADER

RESPECT

NOX PRESS
books for that extra kick to give you more power
www.NoxPress.com

Also by Elise Leonard:

The **JUNKYARD DAN** series: (*Nox Press*)
1. Start of a New Dan
2. Dried Blood
3. Stolen?
4. Gun in the Back
5. Plans
6. Money for Nothing
7. Stuffed Animal
8. Poison, Anyone?
9. A Picture Tells a Thousand Dollars
10. Wrapped Up
11. Finished
12. Bloody Knife
13. Taking Names and Kicking Assets
14. Mercy

THE SMITH BROTHERS (a series): (*Nox Press*)
1. All for One
2. When in Rome
3. Get a Clue
4. The Hard Way
5. Master Plan

A LEEG OF HIS OWN (a series): (*Nox Press*)
1. Croaking Bullfrogs, Hidden Robbers
2. 20,000 LEEGS Under the C
3. Failure to Lunch
4. Hamlette

The **AL'S WORLD** series: (***Simon & Schuster***)
Book 1: Monday Morning Blitz
Book 2: Killer Lunch Lady
Book 3: Scared Stiff
Book 4: Monkey Business

The **LEADER** series: (*Nox Press*)
- ✯ Honor
- ✯ Courage
- ✯ Respect
- ✯ Service
- ✯ Integrity
- ✯ Commitment
- ✯ Loyalty
- ✯ Duty

LEADER

RESPECT

Elise Leonard

NOX PRESS
books for that extra kick to give you more power
www.NoxPress.com

Leonard, Elise
LEADER (a series) / Respect
ISBN: 978-1-935366-26-3

Copyright © 2010 by Elise Leonard.
All rights reserved, including the right of reproduction in whole or in part in any form. Published by Nox Press.
www.NoxPress.com

First Nox Press printing: April 2010

books for that extra kick to give you more power

**This book is dedicated to
the Patriot Guard Riders.**

To all of those who have served:
Thank you.

To all of those who have the wonderful traits
that are the titles of the books in this series:
Thank you.

The world becomes a better place
when people have these attributes.

So... no matter what the past brought,
or what the present holds,
or what the future brings...
be a LEADER!

~Elise

re-spect –noun

1. esteem for or a sense of the worth or excellence of a person, a personal quality or ability, or something considered as a manifestation of a personal quality or ability: *I have great respect for her judgment.*
2. deference to a right, privilege, privileged position, or someone or something considered to have certain rights or privileges; proper acceptance or courtesy; acknowledgment: *respect for a suspect's right to counsel; to show respect for the flag; respect for the elderly.*
3. the condition of being esteemed or honored: *to be held in respect.*
4. respects, a formal expression or gesture of greeting, esteem, or friendship: *Give my respects to your parents.*

re-spect –Idioms

5. in respect of, in reference to; in regard to; concerning.
6. pay one's respects,
    a. to visit in order to welcome, greet, etc.: *We paid our respects to the new neighbors.*
    b. to express one's sympathy, esp. to survivors following a death: *We paid our respects to the family.*

CHAPTER 1

They say the war in Vietnam was like no other war, past or since.

Paul didn't know about that.

He'd lived through it.

Many did not.

So he guessed that made him one of the lucky ones.

For some, Vietnam had been their worst nightmare.

For Paul, it was not.

Elise Leonard

The war was a piece of cake compared to what he got when he returned home.

And that war was *not* easy!

But neither was what Paul came home to.

The people were mad at the *soldiers*.

They *blamed* the soldiers! (They thought the soldiers *started* the war!)

But Paul didn't like to speak about it.

The past was the past.

He couldn't ignore it.

He couldn't change it.

But he *could* learn from it.

CHAPTER 2

The news blared on the TV.

Paul was deaf in one ear.

In Vietnam, they shot out his cardrum.

But he didn't care.

At least he was still alive.

He'd never gone for a hearing aid.

Why bother?

He lived alone in a small house. So the TV didn't disturb anyone.

"Another local soldier is coming home

from the war in Iraq..." the TV blared.

Paul took his frozen pizza out of the oven.

It wasn't quite done yet.

He stuck it back in.

"*But he will not be walking off the plane that carried him home...*"

Paul looked in his refrigerator.

He took out a soda.

He popped it open.

Then he took a long swig of the cold drink.

"*He is yet one more casualty from this war in Iraq...*"

"Rest in peace, my brother," Paul muttered to himself. "Rest in peace."

The TV was now showing a scene of protest.

Many people were gathered at the airport.

They held signs.

Respect

"NO MORE WAR!" the signs said.

"***NO MORE WAR!***" the people chanted.

Paul frowned.

He sighed a heavy sigh.

"When will these people ever learn?!" he muttered to himself.

Just then the phone rang.

"Yeah?" Paul answered.

(He was never very formal. He figured that if the person calling *knew* him, they'd know that already. And if the person calling *didn't* know him? They'd get to *know* that about him right away.)

CHAPTER 3

"Paul? It's Cory. Looks like we have a job."

Paul's eyes flicked toward the TV.

"Yeah, I figured as much," Paul said.

"You'd think it would stop," Cory said.

"Yeah," Paul said. "You'd think."

"Remember when we came home?" Cory asked Paul.

"How could I forget?"

"When that lady threw that blood on you?

Respect

I didn't know what to do! And when she called us 'baby killers,' I was so shocked!"

"Me too," Paul said.

Paul scratched his chin.

"You know it was red paint. Right? Not blood."

"Yes," Cory said. "But it *symbolized* blood. So to me, it was the same thing."

Paul nodded.

"I guess."

The phone line was quiet for a few moments.

"The parents of this kid are really hurting," Cory said.

"I can understand," Paul replied.

"But it gets worse," Cory said.

Paul waited for it.

"They got a letter from a religious group," Cory explained.

Again, Paul waited for it.

"It said something like, 'Your son's a

killer, he deserved to die.'"

"You're kidding me!" Paul said.

"Nope."

"And they consider themselves to be a religious group?" Paul asked.

"Yup."

Paul shook his head.

Then he sighed loudly.

"I don't get people," Paul said.

"Well, in that letter, they even added that they are *glad* the boy died."

"Please tell me you're kidding me," Paul said.

"Nope. Sorry."

Paul had to ask again.

"They really wrote that to the family of a fallen soldier?"

"Yup," Cory replied.

Paul sighed sadly.

CHAPTER 4

"So when is he coming home?" Paul asked.

"In two days," Cory said.

"And *already* it's a media circus?!" Paul muttered to himself.

"I'm meeting with the parents today," Cory said. "Want to come?"

"If you need me there," Paul said.

"I always need you, bro. You had my back in 'Nam. And you have my back now. I wouldn't trust anyone but you with something like this."

Paul scoffed.

"Then you're in some serious trouble, my friend!" Paul told Cory.

Paul hung up and went back to the oven.

His pizza was ready.

A little overcooked, but Paul didn't mind.

He'd eaten worse.

Like that time in 'Nam when he was forced to eat a raw chicken.

Just broke its neck, and ate it raw.

He couldn't cook it. To start a fire would have been too dangerous.

But he'd run out of rations a long time ago, and was starving.

He knew he needed to eat something. Or he would die soon. But there was not much for him to forage.

Not in that God forsaken place.

Respect

But then, lo and behold, a chicken just happened to cross his path.

Paul took that as a sign from God himself!

He was starving.

He needed food.

He couldn't give up his post. Not without dying.

Yet, if he didn't eat, he'd *also* die.

So he was in a state of panic.

He didn't know what to do!

He didn't know the right choice to make.

Should he leave his post and risk being shot?

Or should he stay at his post and risk death by starvation?

It wasn't an easy choice to make.

He was leaning toward leaving his post.

Dying from a bullet would be fast and quick.

Dying from starvation? Not so fast or

quick.

Plus, Paul thought that might be pretty painful.

Hunger pangs were one thing.

Dying of hunger, another.

So he was almost ready to leave his post.

He was almost ready to risk getting shot. Or worse... capture.

That too would be painful!

But something made him hesitate for just that split second longer.

And a dang *chicken* walked right over to him.

Sure, it was skinny.

It seemed everything and everyone was starving in 'Nam. (Including the chickens.)

But that chicken came *right* to him.

CHAPTER 5

To this day, Paul has trouble seeing a roast chicken.

It brings it all back.

But he's never told anyone.

It would gross them out too much.

It would make people think he was an animal.

But he needed to do it.

To survive.

Unless you were there, you couldn't know

how it was like.

If he hadn't lived it himself, he'd never believe what he'd lived through.

It was like when his buddies told him fishing stories.

Paul never quite believed those stories.

They were too far-fetched.

Too unlikely.

But any Vietnam story he'd heard?

Paul knew they were all true.

It was hard to make up stuff like that.

Who in their right mind would want to?!

It was too horrible.

No one was *that* cold or hard or polluted.

Paul's doorbell rang about an hour later.

It was Cory.

"Ready to speak to the parents?" he asked Paul.

"No," Paul replied.

"You need a little more time? Want to change your clothes?" Cory asked.

Respect

"What's wrong with my clothes?"

Paul looked down at his clothes.

His jeans were the same jeans he'd been wearing for the last ten years.

They were Levi's.

They lasted forever, if you stayed the same size.

There was nothing fancy about them. But they were clean, and Paul thought they looked okay.

Paul looked at his shirt.

His T-shirt was old. But was still good.

It didn't have any holes or anything.

Paul sniffed at his shirt.

"Does it smell or something?" he asked Cory.

"No."

"So why do you think I need to change my clothes?" he asked his friend.

"I never said that," Cory said. "*You* just said you weren't ready to speak to the boy's parents."

Paul looked at Cory.

"I'm never ready," Paul said. "Who can ever be ready to speak with someone's parents about their deceased child?!"

Cory nodded.

"So true, bud. So true," he said.

Paul sighed heavily.

"Okay," Paul said. "Let's go."

CHAPTER 6

The parents were distraught.

There was no other word for it.

To lose one's child is a tragedy.

A parent would rather give their own life, than live to see their child die before them.

It was a hard thing to go through.

Paul's heart ached for them.

"I'm sorry for your loss," he said gently.

The boy's mother was crying.

She wiped her tears with a tissue.

A tissue that was already soaked.

"Thank you," she said softly.

The boy's father was in pain.

But the man was trying to be strong.

Probably for his wife.

Most likely because if he allowed himself? He'd lose it completely.

Paul understood.

They sat in silence for a few moments.

Paul spoke gently.

"I heard you got a letter."

The woman started crying again.

The dad got up.

He walked to the other side of the room.

He went in a small desk.

Then he walked back with the letter.

He handed the letter to Paul.

This was always hard for Paul.

He never knew what to say.

What were you supposed to say in that situation?!

Respect

There really were no words.
So Paul just said the polite thing.
"Thank you," Paul said.
The man nodded quickly.

CHAPTER 7

Paul opened the letter.

It came from a local religious group.

Paul had seen their name and logo before.

A couple of times.

So he knew it came from a real place.

Paul started to read the letter.

It was a hateful letter.

And as Cory had said, it *did* say that they were glad this couple's son was dead.

Respect

Paul was shocked.

It was bad enough to hear about it.

But Paul had hoped that Cory or the parents had misunderstood the meaning of the letter.

But there was no mistake made!

No.

This was straight and to the point.

And very, very hateful.

Paul didn't understand the thinking behind a letter like this.

How could anyone *say* something like this?!

"Do you know this place?" Paul asked the couple.

"No."

"Did they know your son?" Paul asked.

"No."

"Do they know *you*?" Paul asked.

"No."

Paul didn't get it!

He didn't get anything *about* this.

Like, for example... how could these people think they were religious?!

To tell the parents of a dead child that they are *happy*?

And that a boy *deserved* to die?

A boy who was only doing his job?

A boy who was in service for the United States?

As far as Paul knew, the boy didn't *start* the war.

The boy didn't *instigate* the war.

Paul didn't even know if the boy *believed* in the war.

But the boy was a serviceman.

A proud soldier.

Doing his duty.

Serving the United States.

Doing it with courage. And integrity. And commitment. And loyalty.

The boy had put his *life* on the line.

Respect

He had done his duty.

He had done what he was *told* to do.

And because of that, he died.

What kind of religion was happy to see a young boy die?!

Paul wiped his hand over his face.

He sighed deeply.

Paul just didn't get where this kind of thing came from.

CHAPTER 8

Paul spoke gently.

"I'm sorry that they said this to you."

"Thank you," the boy's mother said.

"We won't let them near you," Paul said. He smiled gently.

"The Patriot Guard Riders will do whatever it takes."

"Thank you," she said again.

"What do you do, exactly?" the boy's father asked.

Respect

"That's a good question," Paul said.

He smiled sadly.

"We help the families of fallen soldiers," Paul said.

"We are all vets," Cory added.

"We will stand guard around your house."

Paul grimaced.

"No one will get in who is not invited."

"Thank you," the man said.

"Then we will escort you to the funeral," Paul said.

"That would be great."

"We will make sure that you are not disturbed at the funeral," Paul said.

A soft sigh escaped from the boy's mother.

"That will be wonderful," she said.

Paul lowered his voice.

"And then we will escort your son's body to the burial."

The father nodded.

It looked like he was trying not to cry.

It was taking every bit of will-power.

But the man was trying to stay strong.

"Thank you," he choked out.

"You don't have to thank us," Paul said.

"Yes," he said. "We do."

"Those people said they were going to come to the funeral," the boy's mother said.

"And 'teach us a lesson,'" the father said.

He was trying to control his feelings.

But he was angry and sad.

His emotions were storming within him.

Paul understood.

He would feel the same way.

"Those people will not get near you," Paul said.

"We promise," Cory said.

"You will have enough to deal with on that day," Paul added.

Respect

"Thank you so much for all of your help," the woman said.

The boy's father pointed to the letter.

"I can't believe we even have to worry about all of this," he said.

He looked at Paul.

"You'd think losing my son is enough to go through," he added.

Paul nodded.

"You'd think."

CHAPTER 9

"We got other letters, too," the boy's mom said.

Paul got angry.

"Like *that* one?!" Paul roared.

"No. No. Good letters. *Nice* letters," she said.

She looked at her husband.

He nodded.

Then he walked to the desk.

He pulled out more letters.

Respect

The letters were tied together with a ribbon.

It was clear that the parents would save those letters.

The father handed the letters to Paul.

He opened the first one. The one on the top.

Dear Mr. and Mrs. Snyder,

You don't know me.

But I was one of your son's friends.

We were in the Iraq war together.

Your son saved my life.

More than once.

He saved me a number of times.

And I wasn't the only one he saved.

He saved a lot of us guys.

Michael was smart. He looked out for all of us.

One night a bomb went off near our barracks.

We were all sleeping.

So we would have all been dead.

But Michael was up.

And he heard the bomb come in.

He screamed to wake us up.

He screamed, "***Gas! Gas! Get your masks on! NOW!***"

So we all woke up and put on our gas masks.

He saved all of us that day!

I just wanted to write to say I am sorry for your loss.

I am sorry for our loss. But it must be harder for you, his parents.

Michael was well liked!

Someone once said: All gave some. Some gave all.

Michael gave all.

And then it was signed.

CHAPTER 10

"That's a nice letter," Paul said.

"Yes," Mrs. Snyder said.

"And there are more. Please, read on," Mr. Snyder said.

Paul folded up the letter.

He put it back in the envelope.

Then he took out another letter.

This one looked like it was written by a girl.

The writing was big and loopy.

To Paul, it looked like a girl's handwriting.

He looked at the name on the bottom of the letter.

Diala.

Yes, that was a girl's name.

He read the letter.

Dear Mr. and Mrs. Snyder,

I was deployed with your son, and served with him.

He was a good man.

We were trained together.

And he always helped me out.

There was this one time. We were told what to do if we were in a SCUD missile attack.

We had to practice what we were taught. (So we would be safe.)

We had to learn how to put on our gas masks.

We had to learn how to put on our chemical

Respect

protection suits.

We had to do it quickly.

If not, we could die from chemical or biological agents.

We only had nine seconds to put it all on.

After those nine seconds, we ran the risk of exposure and death.

So we had to be quick.

I could not get my suit and mask on that quickly.

Nine seconds is not a long time.

But Michael did not give up on me.

He made me practice.

Over and over.

He made me do it again and again.

And then again.

Until I could get my mask and suit on in under nine seconds.

It was a good thing that he did that.

Because soon after, we were hit!

Sirens blared.

Everyone was running around.

People were screaming.

Running for their lives.

Trying to get their suits on.

Trying to get their masks on.

"***SCUD missile attack!***" we all yelled.

And within seconds, my mask was on.

Seconds later, my suit was on.

The pants, the coat, the gloves and the boots.

I did it all in under nine seconds.

And I did it because Michael forced me to practice.

It was because of him that I was prepared.

It was because of Michael that I lived through that attack.

That one, and the many others that followed.

We'd had so many SCUD alerts. It was almost funny!

Respect

But not really.

In reality, it was scary.

For me, at least.

With each alert, we had to get back into our suits.

At times, I was dog tired!

We also had to wear our body armor.

And our helmets.

And our other gear.

So we were really hot out in the desert!

And we were in a tent. So that made things even worse!

You could drink through the mask.

But you couldn't eat.

So at one time, my body started to shut down.

So did the other soldiers.

I could see them around me.

We were all starting to drop like flies.

Heat exhaustion was one reason.

Lack of food was the other.

"***We can make it!***" Michael had called to all of us

I didn't believe him.

"***Just wait for the 'All Clear' call!***" he shouted. "***You can make it to the All Clear!***"

CHAPTER 11

Paul kept reading the letter...

Then the All Clear was given.
And Michael was right.
I *could* make it!
And I did!
We all did.
We looked like hell.
All of us.
Even Michael.

Elise Leonard

And as soon as we could, we ate.

We got our strength back.

We got our heads together.

And we were once again a strong team.

We owed our survival to your son.

It was Michael who got us through that day.

And many days after that, too.

He was a good soldier.

And he was a good man.

He will be missed.

~Diala

CHAPTER 12

Paul moved on to the next letter.

To the parents of Michael Snyder:

Your son was a fellow soldier. And a friend.
He was a good soldier.
And a good friend.
He was in charge of our convoy.
And he kept us safe.

When a truck would break down? He'd stop the whole convoy.

Mine was one of those trucks that broke down.

And your son saved all of us.

We were stuck. We were sitting ducks.

We were a giant target.

My truck was getting fixed. But it took time.

So Michael got guys out of the trucks.

He made them post security.

At first I thought it wasn't needed.

All I saw were camels and sheep. And oil pipelines.

I saw old, wrecked Iraqi military equipment.

It was just deserted.

It was left right where it was destroyed.

I didn't think there would be a problem.

That was before the insurgent attacks began.

Respect

That was before the insurgents started hitting our U.S. forces.

So we had no clue that danger was lurking.

But Michael did.

And he took steps.

He made sure we were safe.

Which was a good thing.

Because the insurgents surprised us.

Out of nowhere, they appeared.

They surrounded us.

If it weren't for Michael's posts? We'd all be dead now.

Paul couldn't read the signature.

CHAPTER 13

Paul's mind flashed to Vietnam.

It did that sometimes.

He had no control over it.

But Paul was once again in 'Nam.

He was back in his US M113 APC.

Their armored personnel carrier.

His M60s were in the hatch.

The .50 caliber machine gun hatch was open.

And the gunner was on guard.

Respect

At about 0300, 82mm mortars rained down.

It was three in the morning. So the guys were caught off guard.

One mortar landed right on top.

It destroyed an M60. And was only a few inches from coming inside.

Paul woke up.

He was startled.

At first he thought he was in hell.

Maybe he'd died in his sleep.

But no, he wasn't dead.

Someone outside was yelling.

"Don't go out! Don't go out!"

So they'd stayed inside.

The noise was like thunder! But right next to Paul's ears.

Paul's hearing was shot.

He had some shrapnel in his chest and his leg.

The pain took his breath away.

A small piece of shrapnel pierced Paul's eardrum.

Paul waited for the noise to stop.

Then he went outside.

He looked around.

He could not believe his eyes.

The entire place was torn up.

There were mortar shells all over the place.

The fact that he'd survived was a miracle.

He called in about the wounded.

"Gather the wounded," he was told.

"Yes, sir," Paul replied.

"Bring them to the road."

"Yes, sir," Paul repeated.

"The dust-off will land and get you."

"Thank you, sir," Paul said.

Paul gathered the wounded.

One by one he dragged them to the road.

It was a long trip.

Respect

But he did it.
Over and over again.
Paul started with the ones least hurt.
Then moved on to the ones most hurt.
Then he carried over the dead.
He did not want to leave them there.

CHAPTER 14

His leg was bleeding.

It was dragging behind him.

His chest was caked with blood.

His breath was shallow.

He could barely breathe.

But Paul refused to stop.

He wanted to help his men.

He would not stop until all of his men were by the road.

He would not leave a man behind.

Respect

His ear was killing him.

It felt like a hot poker was jabbed in his ear.

But Paul didn't care.

He would keep at it.

He would not stop.

Not until all of his men were safe.

The dust-off found them.

Not one man was conscious.

They were all passed out or dead.

Every single man.

CHAPTER 15

Paul had woken up in the hospital.

He was in bad shape.

But he was better than some of his friends.

He'd remembered carrying some of the dead to the road.

Paul begged the nurses.

"Please tell me about my men."

They didn't want to tell him.

Not until he was strong enough to handle

Respect

it.

Another day would pass.

"Please tell me about my men," Paul asked again.

They would not tell him.

He asked them every day.

"In due time," they would say.

So he kept on asking.

And they kept on putting him off.

But then they finally told him.

"You are strong enough now," one nurse had said.

And then she told Paul.

Paul's chest got tight.

His heart started thumping.

He thought he'd die right then and there.

"*All of them*?!" Paul wailed.

"Yes," the nurse said calmly.

"They're *all* gone?!" he asked.

"Yes, Paul. I'm sorry."

A sound had come from his mouth.

It didn't sound human.

Not even to his ears.

And he was the one who'd made the sound.

"How can that *be*?!" he'd asked them.

"Your efforts got them here," the nurse had said.

Then she'd looked at the floor.

"But we couldn't save them," she'd whispered.

Paul had felt empty inside.

"We tried, Paul. But we couldn't save them. You were the only one we could save."

CHAPTER 16

"Are you okay?" Mr. Snyder asked Paul.

"Oh. Yes. Sorry," Paul said. "Every now and then I sort of zonc out."

"Flash back to the war?" he asked.

"Yes."

"I do that too," he said.

"I think many of us do," Paul replied.

Paul looked at the pile of letters in his hand.

He went back to reading.

Elise Leonard

He took out another letter.

Dear Mr. and Mrs. Snyder,

I served with your son.
He made me proud to be a soldier.
Iraq wasn't about just bombs. Or bullets. Or body counts.
It was about the people we helped, too.
And we helped a lot.
We rebuilt hospitals.
We fixed water systems.
And your son was always there.
Bullets and rockets flew all around us.
Blood was everywhere.
But Mike stayed the course!
I will never forget him.
He was a good man.

And then it was signed.

Respect

"He *was* a good man," Paul said softly.

"Yes," the boy's mother said.

"He deserves respect," Paul said.

"Yes he does," Mr. Snyder said.

"I will make sure he gets it," Paul said.

Then Paul looked at Cory.

"*We* will make sure he gets it," Paul corrected.

CHAPTER 17

The funeral was two days later.

Paul woke up and showered.

He put on his best clothes.

They were not fancy. But they were clean.

Then he put on his leather vest.

It had many patches.

One from Vietnam.

One from the Patriot Guard Riders.

One from his Harley club.

Respect

And there were many more.

They reminded him of who he was.

They told a story.

A story of where he'd been.

What he'd done.

To many, it explained why he was the way he was.

So he wore his vest with pride.

He had to prepare his bike next.

Paul went out to his Harley.

He shined it up.

He put the flag on the back.

It was a huge American flag.

It flew with pride when he rode.

Waving behind him.

Snapping in the wind.

Some people didn't like his flag.

Not that they didn't like the *flag*.

They didn't like that it was on the back of a Harley.

They thought it was disrespectful.

That made him laugh.

If *anyone* had respect for the flag? It was Paul.

And as far as *he* was concerned? They could blow it out their ears.

He'd risked his *life* for this country!

He lost all of his *friends* for this country!

He'd served three tours in *hell* for this country.

So who were *they* to tell *him* he was being disrespectful?!

And usually? The people who said those things? They hadn't served a day in their lives.

CHAPTER 18

Paul drove to the Snyder's house.

He got there early.

He wanted to get there before the people who *didn't* belong got there.

That "religious" group.

Once again, Paul shook his head.

His blood pressure went up.

Just by thinking about what they had said.

We are glad your son is dead! He

deserved to die!

"Try getting by me!" Paul muttered.

He saw his other friends.

They were the Patriot Guard Riders.

They came over to Paul.

"I hope this one's easy," one guy said.

He was a huge guy.

Big and bulky.

He looked like he lifted weights.

"Nope," Paul said. "Most likely not."

The man looked angry.

"These war protestors. They don't get it!" he said.

"I know," Paul said.

"It's not the soldiers' fault," he said.

"I know," Paul said.

"*They* don't start the war," he said.

"I know," Paul said.

"So why do they call us baby killers and stuff?!"

"I don't know," Paul said.

Respect

"When you came home? And they threw that paint on you? I wanted to *kill* them!"

Paul laughed.

"You always were a hot head, Denny!"

"You deserved better than that," Denny said.

"Maybe so," Paul said. "But so does this boy. And his family, too."

"That's why we're here, Paul."

"Yup," Paul said. "That's why we're here."

CHAPTER 19

They came soon after.
They had signs.
They had megaphones.
They had slogans.
Their signs said:
JESUS WOULD NEVER JOIN THE MILITARY
and
STOP WAR
and

Respect

WAR IS DEATH
and the most absurd...
WHO WOULD JESUS BOMB

"They're kidding, right?" Denny said.

He started stomping over to the people with the signs.

Paul caught up with Denny.

"We're here to give the family some peace. Some dignity. Not start a street fight," Paul said.

Denny huffed.

"Yeah. Okay, Paul."

Paul sent Denny back to the line.

The Patriot Guard Riders formed a giant circle around the Snyder's house.

It was a barrier. A line.

One they would not let these people cross.

Then Paul walked over to the people.

"Why are you here?" he asked them.

"We have every right to be here," a lady said.

She was holding the WHAT WOULD JESUS BOMB sign.

"Yes," Paul said. "It's a free country."

"That's right," she said.

"So these people have the right to mourn the loss of their son," Paul said evenly.

"We're not stopping them," she said.

"Yeah," another protester said. "We're glad he's dead!"

Then Paul saw that person raise up his megaphone.

Paul knew the guy was about to repeat what he'd just said.

Only this time? He was going to say it through a megaphone.

Paul gave the signal.

In a split second, the sound was deafening.

All of the Patriot Guard Riders started

Respect

their engines.

They were as loud as thunder.

"You want to be heard?" Paul muttered. "Drown *that* out!"

He chuckled as he walked to his bike.

He mounted his Harley.

He started it.

It roared up.

"Go ahead," Paul muttered. "Spew your hate stuff now!"

CHAPTER 20

It was time to go to the funeral.

The Patriot Guard Riders got together.

They made a wall around the family.

They made sure the family didn't see the signs.

They made sure the family didn't hear the chants.

They kept things calm.

They kept things dignified.

They kept the family safe.

Respect

Safe from mean words.

Safe from mean thoughts.

Safe from unfair thoughts.

Michael Snyder was a good man.

He was doing his job.

He did his job well.

He saved a lot of lives.

He did not kill any babies.

He did not kill innocent people.

He brought peace to a place that had problems.

He made people safe.

He watched out for his own.

He watched out for others.

He rebuilt hospitals.

He helped people get clean water.

He helped feed people.

Hungry people.

He rebuilt schools.

He gave comfort to those who were lost.

He helped those who were in trouble.

He helped people survive missile attacks.

He gave people hope.

He gave people strength.

He gave people dignity.

He gave people respect.

He gave people courage.

He did his duty.

He honored people.

And he deserved a hero's welcome home.

CHAPTER 21

They say the war in Vietnam was like no other war, past or since.

Paul didn't know about that.

He'd lived through it.

Many did not.

So he guessed that made him one of the lucky ones.

For some, Vietnam had been their worst nightmare.

For Paul, it was not.

The war was a piece of cake compared to what he got when he returned home.

And that war was *not* easy!

But neither was what Paul came home to.

The people were mad at the *soldiers*.

They *blamed* the soldiers! (They thought the soldiers *started* the war!)

But Paul didn't like to speak about it.

The past was the past.

He couldn't ignore it.

He couldn't change it.

But he *could* learn from it.

He wished everyone else had learned from it as well.

We hope you liked this book in the

LEADER

series.

We hope you will read
all the books in the series:

HONOR
COURAGE
RESPECT
SERVICE
INTEGRITY
COMMITMENT
LOYALTY
DUTY

Want comedies?

Try reading...

THE SMITH BROTHERS

NOX PRESS
books for that extra kick to give you more power
www.NoxPress.com

We also have...

the very funny

A LEEG OF HIS OWN

series.

NOX PRESS
books for that extra kick to give you more power
www.NoxPress.com

Everyone has it
within them
to be a

LEADER

Do you?

NOX PRESS

books for that extra kick to give you more power
www.NoxPress.com